Do You Hear Them, Daddy?

Written by
Andrea Godfrey Brown
and
Lloyd Herring

Illustrated by
Debbie Gremmelsbacher

Published by Rocking Chair Stories, LLC
Cuba, Missouri
ISBN: 978-0-9889892-0-7

Dedication

To Andy whose curiosity and love for all creatures inspires us daily.

Authors' Note

Boldface and upper case type indicate the authors' effort to mimic the animal sound depicted. Please use them for emphasis as you read.

"Why are you out of bed again, Andy?"

"Daddy, I can't sleep. It's too noisy outside."

"Come over here, and tell me about it."

"I can't sleep. The owls, bats, and frogs are making too much noise!" complained Andy.

"I hear the owl calling, `**Hoot. Hoot.**´

The bat is **Swooshing**.

The frog says, `**Ribbit. Ribbit!**´"

"Do you hear them, Daddy?"

"I hear something, but it's not just noise to me.

Why don't you tell me exactly what you hear, Andy."

"Daddy, everybody knows an owl calls,

`**Hoot, Hoot**.'"

Daddy suggested, " I think you hear a barred owl, but I hear him singing, `**oooh-oooh-oooh-OOOOH! oooh-oooh-oooh-OOOOH!**´"

"Do bats make a noise, Daddy?"

"They chirp like a bird, even though they are flying mammals. They chirp, `**EEEEEEKKK.**'"

"Oh," Andy replied, thinking.

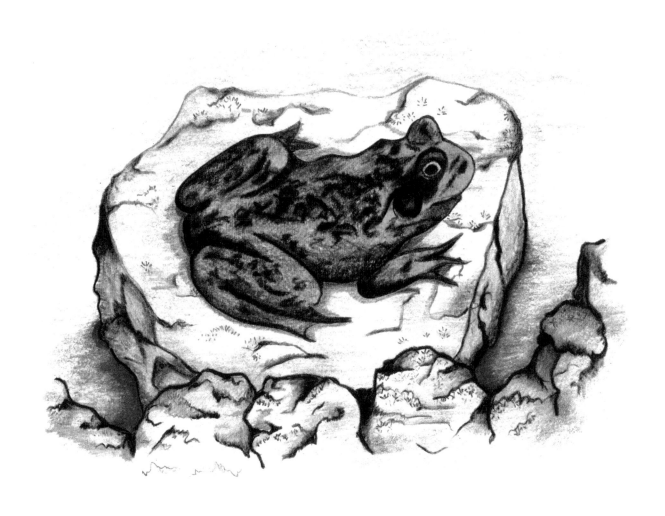

"A frog yelled, `**Ribbit, Ribbit.**´ He kept me awake, too, Daddy!"

"Andy, are you sure he wasn't singing in his deep bull frog voice, `**RUUH-ah–RUUH-ah– RUUH-ah**´?"

"Daddy, what other animals sing at night?"

asked Andy.

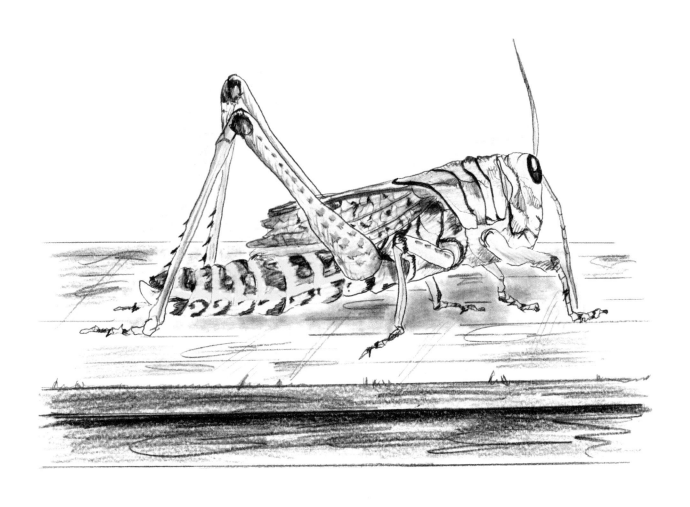

"A cricket is a little bug with a big sound," Daddy

explained. "He sings, `**seet-seet-seet-SEET,**

seet-seet-seet-SEET.´"

"Andy, did you know that coyotes like to howl at night with their friends? They really yip it up!"

"ruh-OOOOOOOH-yip-yip-yip,

ruh-OOOOOOOH-yip-yip-yip,"

Daddy howled.

"Mice squeak their song, Andy.

`**EEEEEEET, EEEEEEET,**'" squeaked Daddy.

"Andy, it's getting late. Let's go back to your room and see what other sounds we can hear together."

"Daddy, what animal sounds like, `**Peet,**

Peet, Peet´?"

"Those are red-eyed tree frogs," Daddy answered.

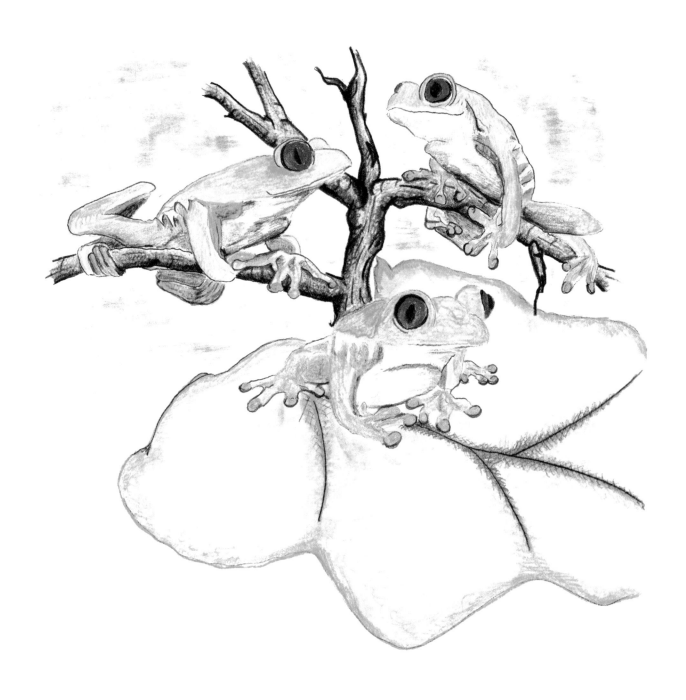

"Those frogs are really little, but when lots of them sing, they are so loud!" Daddy added.

"Did you know that there is a bird who sings its own name, Andy?"

"No. What's its name, Daddy?"

"Its name is Whip-poor-will. It sings this:

`**Whip-per-WIILL, Whip-per-WIILL,**

Whip-per-WIILL.'"

"Good night, Andy. The nighttime creatures
will sing while you sleep. I DO hear their true music,
and I know you do, too."

The End

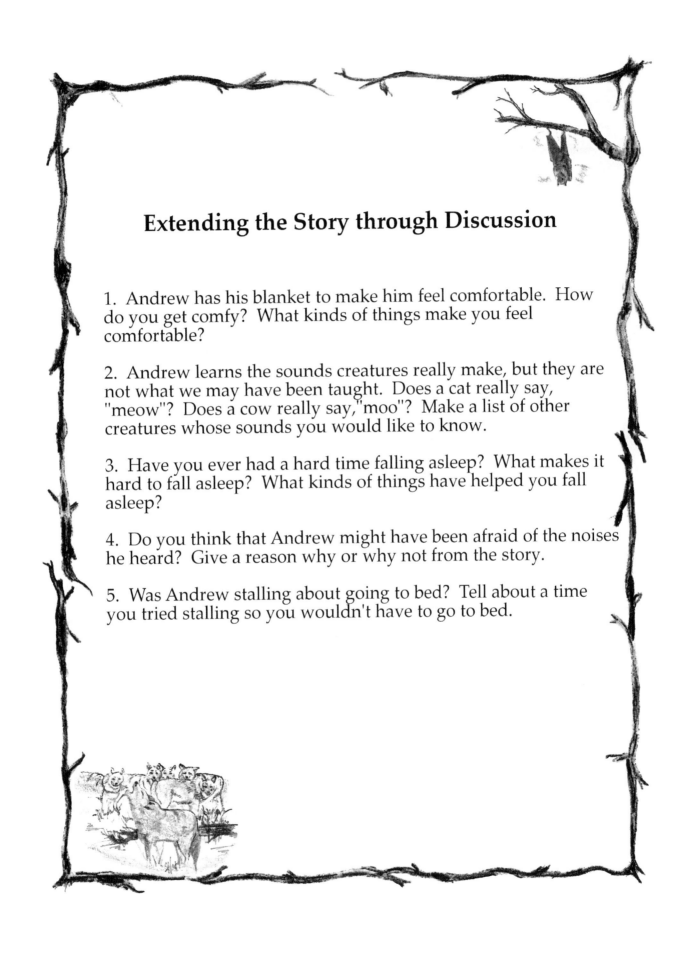

Extending the Story through Discussion

1. Andrew has his blanket to make him feel comfortable. How do you get comfy? What kinds of things make you feel comfortable?

2. Andrew learns the sounds creatures really make, but they are not what we may have been taught. Does a cat really say, "meow"? Does a cow really say, "moo"? Make a list of other creatures whose sounds you would like to know.

3. Have you ever had a hard time falling asleep? What makes it hard to fall asleep? What kinds of things have helped you fall asleep?

4. Do you think that Andrew might have been afraid of the noises he heard? Give a reason why or why not from the story.

5. Was Andrew stalling about going to bed? Tell about a time you tried stalling so you wouldn't have to go to bed.

Extending the Story through Learning

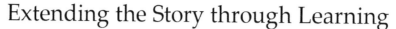

In the story, Andrew learns about the sounds each animal makes. You might like to learn more about the eight animals in the book.

Barred Owl A large owl that lives in North America. We know it is a Barred Owl because of its round head, no ear tufts, brown eyes, yellow beak, dark rings around eyes, and its call. Adults reach a height of 40-63 cm (16-25 in). When the Barred Owl extends its wings, its wingspan is 96-125 cm (38-49 in). Barred Owls usually weigh between 500-1050 grams (1.1-2.3 lbs). The barred owl is a carnivore or meat-eater. Its prey consists of voles, mice, shrews, rats, squirrels, rabbits, bats, and even other smaller birds. They will also wade into the water to capture fish, turtles, and frogs. They even forage for salamanders, snakes, crickets, and beetles.

Fruit Bat The fruit bat is one of the most popular bats in the world. One reason is that their face is cute and looks like a young fox. Sometimes the fruit bat is called the flying fox. All bats are mammals, the only mammal that flies. Fruit bats reach a head and body length of about 2.5 in. (6–7 cm) and a wingspan of about 10 in. (25 cm). The larger fruit bats use their excellent eyesight to find prey, but New World fruit bats are generally smaller and navigate or find their way around by using echolocation or sonar, the same system submarines use underwater. Fruit bats also rely on their nose to find food. Fruit bats eat mostly just fruit and no insects or blood at all. They tend to feed from flower nectar, like butterflies. They do have teeth to bite through the skin of the fruit.

Bullfrog The American Bullfrog is the largest frog in North America. Bullfrogs are amphibians. This means they are cold-blooded, have smooth skin, and a skeleton. They can live on land or in water. Amphibians hatch as a swimming larva with gills. They later transform into adults and use lungs to breathe. Bullfrogs are active at night hunting for food. They eat whatever they can swallow such as fish, turtles, rats, bats, and even small water birds. Their sticky mucous covered tongue is super fast and used to strike and capture their prey. They live among the shallow, plant-filled areas of lakes, swamps, and ponds. Male bullfrogs have an inflatable balloon-like pouch under their skin that lets them make their loud croaking calls at night. They have a body length of 3.5-6 inches, and a large mature bullfrog can weigh up to 1.1 lbs.

Cricket Crickets are insects that are harmless to humans. Only male crickets chirp, and the scientific name is stridulation. The sound is created by moving one wing across "teeth" located on the bottom of the other wing. During this process, they also hold their wings up and open which act like mini-amplifiers for their sound. No wonder they can be so loud! Crickets do not make their sounds by rubbing their legs together, even though that's what people think. Most of their sounds relate to attracting females or repelling other males. Crickets hear through a drum-like membrane, called an eardrum, located just below the middle joint of each front leg. Cricket chirps speed up during warmer temperatures, and some scientists who study crickets can tell the temperature by counting the chirps per minute. Crickets are omnivores. They eat vegetation and meat. They feed on decaying plants, fungi, or other dead crickets.

Coyote The coyote is a mammal that lives in North, Central, and South America. They are about the size of a medium-sized dog. They often have a litter of about 6 pups. Their coloring varies greatly from grey brown to brownish yellow depending on where they live. A coyote can reach a short running speed of about 40 miles per hour. Coyotes are similar to wolves and are believed to have come from the European grey wolf. Coyote ears are very large compared to the size of their head, so they have excellent hearing, even better than dogs! Their communication consists of yips, yelps, and barks. The yips are a series of short notes and are most often heard at dusk or night. Coyotes travel in packs and are generally nocturnal or active at night. They prefer to hunt for food in mated pairs. Coyotes are not as social as wolves but do hunt in packs if the prey is large. They are carnivores and primarily eat small mammals such as voles, prairie dogs, rabbits, ground squirrels, and mice.

Mouse A mouse is a mammal in the rodent order. The best-known mouse species is the common house mouse, and because of its small size and quiet temperament, it is also a popular pet. This small rodent is spread widely throughout nearly every country across the entire planet, even parts of Antarctica! Mice are common prey for many other animals, such as owls, coyotes, and snakes. They can be harmful pests for farmers, damaging crops and spreading disease. Their color varies widely. Each tiny little mouse toe has a fingernail which allows them to climb very well. They can scamper forward and backward easily which helps them avoid predators. Their teeth are sharp and strong and grow continuously, so mice must gnaw them down regularly, stopping overgrowth.

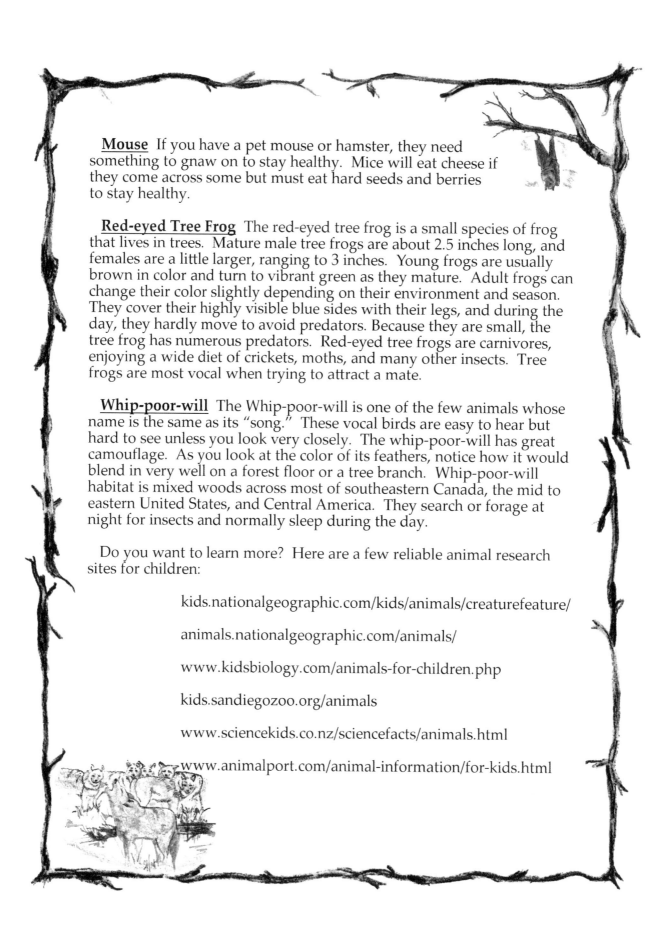

Mouse If you have a pet mouse or hamster, they need something to gnaw on to stay healthy. Mice will eat cheese if they come across some but must eat hard seeds and berries to stay healthy.

Red-eyed Tree Frog The red-eyed tree frog is a small species of frog that lives in trees. Mature male tree frogs are about 2.5 inches long, and females are a little larger, ranging to 3 inches. Young frogs are usually brown in color and turn to vibrant green as they mature. Adult frogs can change their color slightly depending on their environment and season. They cover their highly visible blue sides with their legs, and during the day, they hardly move to avoid predators. Because they are small, the tree frog has numerous predators. Red-eyed tree frogs are carnivores, enjoying a wide diet of crickets, moths, and many other insects. Tree frogs are most vocal when trying to attract a mate.

Whip-poor-will The Whip-poor-will is one of the few animals whose name is the same as its "song." These vocal birds are easy to hear but hard to see unless you look very closely. The whip-poor-will has great camouflage. As you look at the color of its feathers, notice how it would blend in very well on a forest floor or a tree branch. Whip-poor-will habitat is mixed woods across most of southeastern Canada, the mid to eastern United States, and Central America. They search or forage at night for insects and normally sleep during the day.

Do you want to learn more? Here are a few reliable animal research sites for children:

kids.nationalgeographic.com/kids/animals/creaturefeature/

animals.nationalgeographic.com/animals/

www.kidsbiology.com/animals-for-children.php

kids.sandiegozoo.org/animals

www.sciencekids.co.nz/sciencefacts/animals.html

www.animalport.com/animal-information/for-kids.html

Extending the Story through Trying Something New

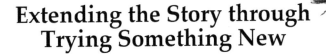

In the story, Andrew complained the animals made noises outside his bedroom window which kept him awake. Here are some things you could try if some sound is keeping you awake.

1. Learn to think about the noises you are hearing in a different way. By talking to his Dad, Andrew learns about the animal noises he hears. He learns what the animal voices really sound like and that the animals are communicating with one another. His Dad helps him think differently about the sounds. He sees that instead of trying to keep him awake, the animals are singing him a nighttime lullaby. Now that he understands the sounds better, they become a source of comfort singing him to sleep.

2. Get Comfy. Andrew has his favorite blanket to help him feel comfortable. Do you have a favorite blanket or stuffed animal to sleep with? Don't overcrowd your space, but get comfy. You can even use your imagination. You could imagine yourself sleeping on a big fluffy cloud or on a raft in still water.

3. Relax your body. Take deep breaths, 5 seconds in, 5 seconds out, slowly. Watch your belly rise and fall with your breaths for a little while. Next, lying flat on your back, take a deep breath and tense or tighten all the muscles in your body. Then slowly let the breath out, and starting with your toes, release your tensed muscles by going limp. Start with your toes then your knees, hips, tummy, shoulders, and neck.

4. Pay attention to what you eat before bedtime. It is difficult to fall asleep if you are too hungry or if you are too full. Carbohydrates, bananas, and milk-based drinks help us to sleep. Try not to eat high protein foods or spicy foods before bedtime, like meat or barbeque chips. And, of course, don't eat or drink sugary or caffeinated foods close to bedtime.

5. Control the noise closest to you. In the story, Andrew says he is kept awake by the animals making noises outside his bedroom window. If there are inconsistent noises, (noises that start, then stop, then start again) from outside or inside your house, you can cover them up with a **consistent regular noise** closer to you. For example, soft music or even the gentle whir from a fan can often help.

About the Authors

Andrea, Lloyd, and Debbie met while teaching at a St. Louis suburban public high school. Years of cross-departmental professional development bloomed into a friendship, which included Debbie's husband, Gery. These bonds grew as they fished, cooked, and laughed together in their retirement.

Authors Andrea Godfrey Brown and Lloyd Herring are married, having met while teaching high school English. They live on a farm in rural Missouri, along with four horses and a German shepherd. Both are avid fishermen and like nothing more than "dipping a line" into their lake with their sons, daughters-in-law, and grandsons.

Debbie Gremmelsbacher is a National Board Certified physics teacher and a lifelong conservationist. Art has been a long-time interest leading to a series of paintings based on the Missouri Botanical Garden. Illustrating this book about real animal sounds was a true delight for her.

Made in the USA
Charleston, SC
29 October 2013